Sushi & Samosas

A Trip of Tasty Transformations

Rishma Govani

Tellwell Talent
www.tellwell.ca

ISBN
978-0-2288-4104-3 (Hardcover)
978-0-2288-4103-6 (Paperback)

Sushi & Samosas

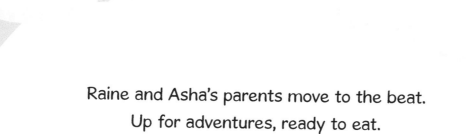

Raine and Asha's parents move to the beat.
Up for adventures, ready to eat.
From home, restaurants, to trucks on the street.

These foodies think global and like to eat local.
But the kids didn't like to try new things, about this they were vocal.
"EW! I'm not in the mood. I don't like new food!"

Little Raine and Asha preferred chicken nuggets and fries,
Crying, "Don't try to hide it. We'll see through your disguise."

Their dad scolded, *"There is more to food than nuggets and fries.
Be grateful. Eat up. The world is yours to recognize."*

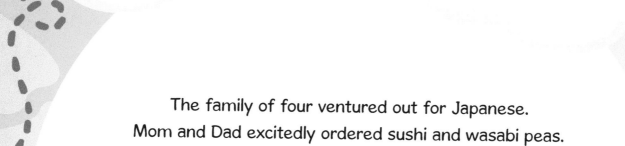

The family of four ventured out for Japanese.
Mom and Dad excitedly ordered sushi and wasabi peas.
Mother sipped miso soup, begging, "Try the tempura, please!"

Brother and sister held tight and refused.
Asha was tempted but the seaweed left her confused.
"NO WAY! I don't want sushi!" said Raine, his chopsticks unused.
But when sister tried a cucumber roll, her taste buds were amused.

Mother smiled and sang, "*The more you go, the more you know.
The more you try, the more you fly!*"

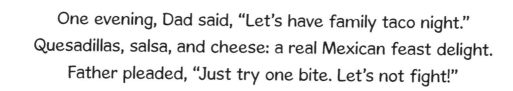

One evening, Dad said, "Let's have family taco night."
Quesadillas, salsa, and cheese: a real Mexican feast delight.
Father pleaded, "Just try one bite. Let's not fight!"

The pair of siblings started to complain and whine.
Raine was curious but the pinto beans didn't appear fine.
Asha exclaimed, "NO! I don't like it," making a quick beeline.
But brother tasted the guacamole. His world spun and began to shine.

Their daddy winked, *"There is more to food than nuggets and fries.*
Be grateful. Eat up. The world is yours to recognize."

On the way home from work, Mom stopped for Greek takeout.
Souvlaki, gyros, and feta make a yummy dinner, no doubt.
"Greek food is here!" she announced with a happy shout.

The hard-to-please team were grumpy, rolling their big brown eyes.
The little sister was hungry but the lamb she despised.
Raine said, "GROSS, no way!" with sad tears and loud sighs.
Then Asha tasted the tzatziki and her eyes lit up to the skies.

Their mommy laughed, "OPA! *The more you go, the more you know.*
The more you try, the more you fly."

One Saturday night, the foodies craved Thai.
Green curry chicken, and tasty soup: Tom Kha Gai.
On the way to the restaurant, the kids kept asking, "Why?"

Bro and Sis weren't budging. They wouldn't eat a thing.
Raine was intrigued but the new smells were overwhelming.
Asha screamed, "That's YUCKY!" and threw down her napkin ring.
Brother caved to the mango salad and his heart began to sing.

Father munched his spring roll and beamed.
*"There is more to food than nuggets
and fries. Be grateful. Eat up. The world is yours to recognize."*

The foursome was invited to a friend's house for dinner.
Hummus, tabbouleh, beef shawarma: this spread was a winner.
Their hungry parents warned, "Don't be a complainer!"

The Middle Eastern feast didn't leave Bro and Sis thrilled.
Asha picked away at her pita bread and shish taouk grilled.
Her brother left the table in favour of games and blocks to build.
Asha tried the falafel and felt fantastically fulfilled.

Their mother high fived, "*The more you go, the more you know.
The more you try, the more you fly!*"

One weekend, off to an Indian wedding the fun family went.
Naan, samosas, and daal, this would be a special event.
On the car ride there, Mom reminded the kids not to vent.

Bright colours and flavourful smells filled the room, oh so nice.
Hungry Raine was worried the food had too much spice.
Asha left to dance after quick bites of biryani rice.
Raine tried the butter chicken, was transformed, and tried it twice!

Their dad fist pumped his son, "*There is more to food than nuggets and fries.*
Be grateful. Eat up. The world is yours to recognize."

Pooped after work one evening, too tired to cook,
Mom and Dad offered nuggets but got a cross look.
Then the duo retrieved their around the world cookbook.

Injera, Kimchi, or Paella, the children were keen to prepare.
Ethiopian, Korean, or Spanish, nothing EW, YUCKY or too rare.

With a refreshed view, the pair embarked on their global flight.
With countless trips to explore, there was never again a food fight.

Asha giggled and reminded, *"There is more to food than nuggets and fries.*
Be grateful. Eat up. The world is yours to recognize."

Raine wagged his finger and laughed,
"Remember the more you go, the more you know.
The more you try, the more you fly!"

ABOUT THE AUTHOR

Rishma Govani has spent the last three decades committed to breaking down barriers, extending bridges, and championing cross-cultural understanding, awareness, and acceptance.

Curious by nature, she is a trailblazing advocate for pluralism. She is the CFO (Chief Food Officer) for TFLC, the Toronto Food Luck Club, a successful dinner club that explored over 100 world cuisines for 15 years in Toronto. TFLC is the inspiration behind this book.

A daughter of Ugandan refugees, trained as a journalist, and known as an eternal optimist, she hopes to contribute to global peace by helping people learn more about the world's diverse cultures. She continues to think global and eat local with the real-life version of Asha & Raine, her children Mila & Khalil Mulji and in honour of their dad, the biggest foodie of them all.

CPSIA information can be obtained
at www.ICGtesting.com
Printed in the USA
LVHW072222030921
696802LV00018B/29